To my family who encouraged me.
To Shukai who inspired me.
And to my grandparents who said I could.

Far, far away
in a dark lonely land,
where a sad little boy sat
and thought of a plan.

A plan to escape the
black smoke and grey smog.
A way to see more than
thick mist and fog.

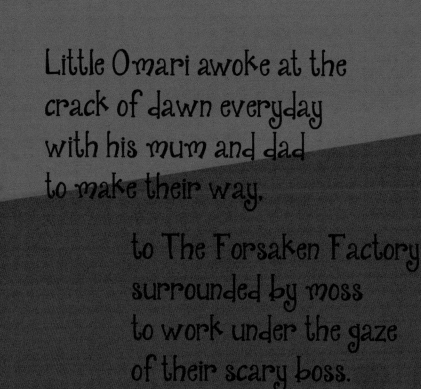

Little Omari awoke at the
crack of dawn everyday
with his mum and dad
to make their way.

to The Forsaken Factory
surrounded by moss
to work under the gaze
of their scary boss.

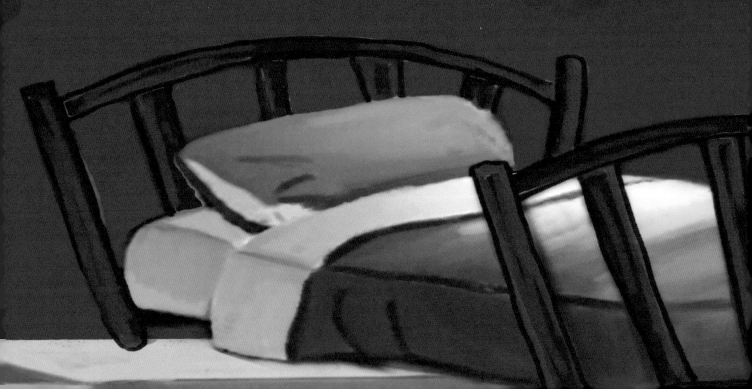

Omari would take his seat and
sew, cut and shear
heaps of clothes until they became
desirable wear.

The factory workers repeated
this day and night,
with only a small dusty window
to give them a pleasant sight.

Over the hills and near the fluffy white clouds, stood an amazing palace so tall and proud. While Omari worked he would stare and dream about life in the palace and its eternal beam.

The palace was set in grass so green,
inhabited by its king and queen.
Its crystal blue floors and
glittery white walls

were not enough to stop
Princess Unique from
not feeling cheerful at all.

The Princess would play on the palace grounds
Surrounded by tall trees and pretty flowers in their mounds
But still the Princess would sit and think at night;"this cannot be it,
I am so lonely,
there must be more to life."

Down in the valley,
little Omari rose for work.
He felt so blue but all of a sudden
his frown turned into a smirk.

Instead of going to the factory
where he felt down,
he made his way to the palace
all the way on the other side of town.

Omari walked, crawled and climbed
over the high hills, murky mountains
and trees filled with slime.
He finally reached
the palace only to find
that he stood alone in
the palace's overwhelming shine.

Just upstairs in her room packed with toys,
the Princess cried as she could not enjoy
her games and laughter
because it was
meant for two.
She took a walk
down the hallway
to a place she longed
for and knew.

In the courtyard, the Princess
got some fresh air.
She felt at peace until
she could hear

the sound of sighs
and quiet cries.
She walked to the sound and
met a little boy's brown eyes.

"I thought I was alone and
my head filled with dread.
"What are you doing in this
lonely place?" Omari said.

"I am Princess Unique and
I wish to share with someone.
Will you stay and play with me?
It'll be so much fun."

Princess Unique and Omari played
for hours and hours
day and night, their joy never turned sour.
When they were alone in the factory or
the palace they did not feel down
because they knew they would
see each other again when the sun
rose and the moon went down.

Over the months their
friendship and bond grew.
Seconds turned to hours
as time flew.

The pair found happiness
in each other's downfall
they learnt you can be grateful
even when you don't have it all.

Printed in Great Britain
by Amazon